My Pinsans & Me

Amara's Talent Show

By Monica Canlas Tuy and Eric Tuy

Illustrated by Joseph Canlas

To our dream girl, Amara:
You inspired us to write this book before you were even born.
We hope it encourages you to dream and do wonderful things.
We love you more than the words could ever reach.

Ding-dong! rang the doorbell.

"Mommy! Daddy! My pinsans are here!" Amara exclaimed.

Ding-dong!

"Lolo! Lola! My cousins are here!"

Kuya Mikey

Subi

Amara

Belle

Bunso

One by one, Amara's pinsans, titos, and titas walked into her house. Everyone brought a delicious Filipino dish to eat for lunch.

Amara pulled her pinsans into a circle.
She twirled around and said,   "Let's perform a dance for Lolo and Lola.
I learned a new dance that I can teach you!"

But her cousins had
other ideas.

"I don't want to dance,"
said Belle.

"I want to sing!"

"But I don't know
how to sing,"
said Amara.

"I don't want to dance," said Ate Melody.

"I want to make the baby laugh!"

But I don't know how to make the baby laugh," said Amara.

"I don't want to dance," said Kaylee

"I want to do gymnastics!"

"But I don't know how to
do gymnastics,"
said Amara.

The pinsans began to argue about which talent they should perform.

Amara wanted to do something special for Lolo & Lola but her cousins could not agree on the same idea.

"Kain na tayo!
It's time to eat!"
said Amara's
nanay and tatay.

The table was filled with Filipino dishes that each family made for lunch.

There was delicious food like...

Sinigang

Adobo

Lumpia

Pancit

and Amara's favorite dessert, Halo-halo.

Lola's words gave Amara a great idea.

"What if we each show our different talents to Lolo and Lola?" asked Amara.

"It will be just like our lunch. Every talent is different, but when you put them all together, they make a very special talent show!"

"Yeah!" exclaimed the pinsans.

They began to practice their special talents and set up the stage for the talent show.

And so the talent show began!

Joey performed his magic tricks,

and Kaylee did her gymnastics!

Ate Melody made the baby laugh,

and Belle sang a song!

Kuya Mikey built a robot,

and Kuya David showed off his jumpshot!

Amara danced across the stage to end the show.

Cheers and applause filled the room. All of the titos and titas were so proud to see everyone's talents.

Lolo and Lola said it was the best talent show they had ever seen!

GALING NAMAN!

The pinsans lined up and took a bow together.
They were proud of themselves, too!

The cousins had different talents but they worked together as a team to put on a very special and fun talent show.

Soon it was time for everyone to go home.

One by one, the pinsans, titos and titas each said goodbye.

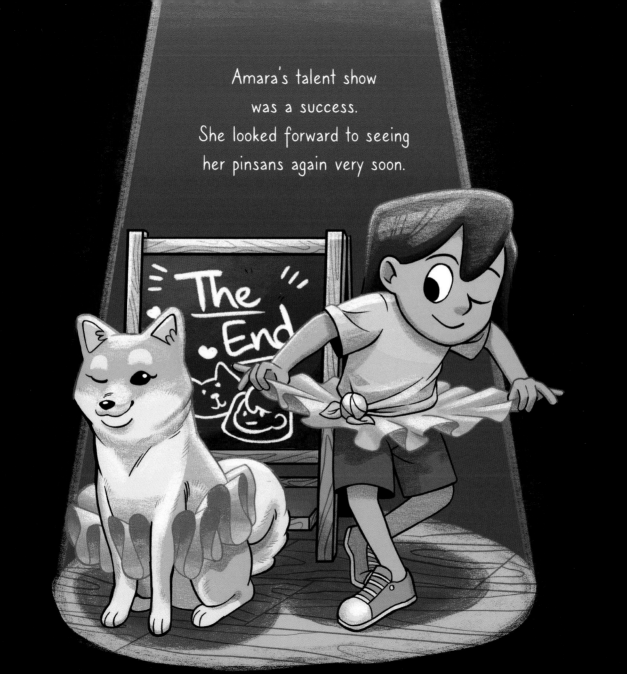

Amara's talent show
was a success.
She looked forward to seeing
her pinsans again very soon.

Glossary

Lola - Grandmother

Lolo - Grandfather

Nanay - Mother

Tatay - Father

Titos - Uncles

Titas - Aunts

Kuya - Older brother, relative, or friend

Ate - Older sister, relative, or friend

Anak - Child

Bunso - Youngest child in the family

Pinsans - Cousins

"Kain na tayo!" - "Let's eat!"

"Galing naman!" - "Excellent!"

Lumpia - Fried spring eggrolls

Pancit - Rice noodles cooked with meat and vegetables

Adobo - Meat dish cooked in soy sauce, vinegar, and garlic

Sinigang - A sour and savory meat or seafood dish

Halo Halo - Dessert made with crushed ice, evaporated milk, ube, sweetened beans, leche flan, and jelly

To request permissions, contact the publisher at thetuys@gmail.com

Hardcover: 978-1-7353493-5-0
Paperback: 978-1-7353493-7-4
Ebook: 978-1-7353493-8-1

First paperback edition January 2022.

Authors: Monica Canlas Tuy and Eric Tuy

Illustrator: Joseph Canlas